The traditional ghost story
is set in a castle
in England.

The ghost is usually that of Lord or Lady Something-or-Other who had his or her head cut off in the fifteenth century. The stories in this book are not traditional. All of them are set in America. Well, one is in Canada, but that's close enough. Most of them are modern—within the last hundred years or so. When it comes to ghosts, that's modern.

The ghosts in this book don't haunt castles, or even graveyards. They can be found in frame houses in Detroit, or airplanes in Florida. And sometimes the ghost is only a phone call away. . . .

Books by Daniel Cohen

THE GREATEST MONSTERS IN THE WORLD
HORROR IN THE MOVIES
THE MONSTERS OF STAR TREK
MONSTERS YOU NEVER HEARD OF
REAL GHOSTS
THE RESTLESS DEAD: Ghostly Tales from Around
    the World
SCIENCE FICTION'S GREATEST MONSTERS
STRANGE AND AMAZING FACTS ABOUT STAR
    TREK
SUPERMONSTERS

Available from ARCHWAY Paperbacks

GHOSTLY TERRORS
THE GHOSTS OF WAR
PHONE CALL FROM A GHOST: Strange Tales from
    Modern America
THE WORLD'S MOST FAMOUS GHOSTS
ZOO SUPERSTARS

Available from MINSTREL BOOKS

PHONE CALL
FROM A
GHOST

DANIEL COHEN

A
MINSTREL®
BOOK

PUBLISHED BY POCKET BOOKS

New York   London   Toronto   Sydney   Tokyo   Singapore

Picture credits: Bell Labs, 14; AP/Wide World Photos, 39, 41. Drawings
by David Linn.

A Minstrel Book published by
POCKET BOOKS, a division of Simon & Schuster Inc.
1230 Avenue of the Americas, New York, NY 10020

ISBN: 0-671-73359-1

First Minstrel Books printing October 1990

10 9 8 7 6

A MINSTREL BOOK and colophon are registered trademarks
of Simon & Schuster Inc.

Printed in the U.S.A.

To Glen Pontier,
a teller of ghostly tales

Contents

Introduction

"Where Do You Get Your Stories?"

I have written a lot of ghost story books. So people often ask me, "Where do you get your stories?"

Well, I don't make them up. I collect them. It seems that a lot of people have had, or said they have had, strange and ghostly experiences. From time to time I have traveled around the country to give talks about ghosts or tell ghost stories. Sometimes, after I have finished my talk, someone will come up to me and say:

"Now I know this sounds crazy. And I've never told anyone else, but . . ."

They will then proceed to tell me some strange experience that they have had, or that they have heard from a friend or member of their family. They figure I'm interested in that sort of story, and they're right.

Actually, lots of people collect ghost stories, and I also collect the books and pamphlets and articles they write. Some are quite serious about ghosts. They try to investigate all the circumstances, check out all the facts. They want to know if the story is real, or just the product of an active imagination and poor memory. Others are more casual about collecting ghost stories. If it's a good story, that's enough. They don't look at the details too closely, because the facts can often spoil a good story. I haunt old bookstores in search of volumes of obscure ghost lore of all sorts.

There are accounts of both types in this book. Some of these cases have been investigated. Others are simply set down as they have been told, and may never have happened at all.

These stories don't prove anything about ghosts and are not meant to. They are presented strictly for your entertainment. Of course, if you do happen to believe them, even for a few moments, they can be that much more entertaining.

The traditional ghost story is set in a castle in England. The ghost is usually that of Lord or Lady Something-or-Other who had his or her head cut off in the fifteenth century. The stories in this book are not traditional. All of them are set in America. Well, one is in Canada, but that's close enough. Most of them are modern—within the last hundred years or so. When it comes to ghosts, that's modern.

The ghosts in this book don't haunt castles, or even graveyards. They can be found in frame houses in Detroit, or airplanes in Florida. And sometimes the ghost is only a phone call away.

1

Phone Call
from a Ghost

Imagine this. The phone rings. You pick it up, and you hear a familiar voice. It's the voice of someone you know, someone who is dead!

That's a pretty scary thought. But it has happened. At least there are a lot of people who say it has happened. There have been so many reports of this type that a couple of investigators, D. Scott Rogo and Raymond Bayless, looked into some of these stories.

Rogo and Bayless talked to a woman they called Patricia Adams, though that's not her real name. Patricia Adams is a well-known actress who didn't want her real name used. Most people who report experiences of this type don't want publicity. Patricia Adams told the researchers a story she remembered from when she was a little girl.

Her mother had a close friend—we will call her Mrs. Jones—who also had a daughter, named Barbara. But this girl was much older than Patricia. She had gone away to college, though she would always come back home for the holidays. In her third year at college Barbara was killed in an automobile accident while driving home for the holidays.

A few years after the accident, Patricia Adams and her mother were visiting the Jones family for Thanksgiving. After dinner the children went into one room, the grown-ups into another. Then the telephone rang. Patricia Adams was nearest to the phone so she picked it up. It was the long-distance operator. She said she had a collect call for Mrs. Jones. It was from her daughter, Barbara.

"This threw me a little bit even as a child, and I said, 'Just a minute.' I went and got my mother's friend. She came to the phone and I stood watching her, because I had heard the name and I thought that maybe somebody was playing a joke on me or her or something. She listened on the phone, turned absolutely white, and fainted."

Later Patricia found out why Mrs. Jones's reaction was so extreme. The voice that came over the phone

Telephone styles have varied over the years, but the mysterious phone calls continue.

sounded exactly like that of her dead daughter. The words she used were familiar as well.

"Mommie, it's me. I need twenty dollars to get home."

It was a phrase the dead girl often used before she came home. It had almost become a family joke. Her mother always sent the twenty dollars.

The phone company had no record of the call.

Rogo and Bayless talked to a young musician named Karl. He also had a strange experience to tell them. While he was growing up he lived with his grand-mother, who was almost completely deaf. When Karl went out, and his grandmother was to be alone, he would leave her with a telephone number where he could be reached.

If she wanted him she would dial the number and say, "This is Karl's grandmother. Would you tell him that I need him home?" The grandmother was so deaf that she couldn't hear if anybody answered the phone or not. She would just repeat the phrase five or six times and hang up.

Karl's grandmother died when he was about six-teen. Two years later he was at the home of his friend Peter. Peter and his family didn't know anything about the old woman's strange way of making calls.

Karl and Peter were in the basement practicing some music. The phone rang upstairs and Peter's mother answered. Then she shouted to the basement:

"Karl, there's an old woman on the phone. She says she's your grandmother and she says she needs you. She just keeps saying it over and over again."

Karl rushed up the stairs and grabbed the phone. But the line was dead.

There are lots of accounts where the figure of a person who had just died appears suddenly to a relative or close friend, who may be some distance away.

Sometimes it seems the newly dead person just phones.

Don Owens of Toledo, Ohio, wrote of his experience to *Fate* magazine, a popular publication on psychic topics.

Owens had a close friend named Lee Epps. Though Epps had long held a good job, he lived alone and was basically a shy and lonely man. He was very attached to Owens, and his wife Ethyl, whom he called "Sis."

On the evening of October 28, 1968, the phone rang at the Owens' house. Don Owens was out, but his wife picked up the phone. She recognized Epps's voice immediately. He sounded urgent, and the message was upsetting:

"Sis, tell Don I'm feeling real bad. Never felt this way before. Tell him to get in touch with me the minute he comes in. It's important, Sis."

When Don Owens came home he tried to call his friend. There was no answer. Later that night he learned that Lee Epps had been in the hospital just a few blocks from where the Owens family lived. He had been in a deep coma. He died at 10:30 P.M., the very time the phone call had come in. Doctors agree that there was no way that Epps could have regained consciousness and made the phone call before he died.

The director Alfred Hitchcock was a master of mystery and terror in films and on television. But he loved real-life mysteries as well. In 1955 he wrote an article called "My Five Greatest Mysteries." One of them concerned a very strange phone call.

The event took place in January of 1934. Twenty-year-old Arnie Gandy's parents knew he was in San Francisco. They were expecting a call from him. So when the phone in their New York apartment rang at 3:00 A.M. they were not too surprised. It would be only midnight in California.

The voice Arnie's mother heard was not one she recognized:

"The kid is here and for God's sake forgive him and give him another chance. What I said about him in my letter is all true. He's a fine kid."

Arnie's mother asked who was speaking but the caller didn't give a name. She insisted it must be the wrong number, but the caller repeated the number and it was correct—and their number was unlisted.

She asked to talk to her boy. The caller replied:

"Your son is in a hospital in San Francisco. He's in bad shape. But never mind. He's on his way home now."

There was the sound of other voices in the room, and some laughter. Then another voice—which sounded like Arnie's—said:

"I'm helpless. Here I lie propped up on pillows. I can't move." There was a groan and the line went dead.

Arnie's frantic mother contacted the operator, who assured her that the call had indeed come from San Francisco. Arnie's father contacted the police, who were unable to trace the call.

The next morning Arnie Gandy's body was found in San Francisco Bay. He had been dead for at least two days—well before the mysterious phone call had been placed. The letter the mysterious caller said he had written never arrived.

There was a genuine mystery concerning the boy's death. He had signed onto a ship in New York as mess boy for a world cruise. When the ship docked in San Francisco, Arnie went ashore and never returned. He did not take his clothes or any personal effects from the ship.

That same day he wrote a cheerful letter to his parents, with no indication that anything was wrong. He was never seen again until his body was fished out of the water six days later.

Despite a careful investigation there were no clues

as to why Arnie Gandy left the ship, where he had spent his last days, whether his death was accident, suicide, or murder, or who had made the mysterious phone call.

Hitchcock commented that this was one of the most puzzling real-life mysteries ever. "If I made it into a movie" he said, "no one would believe it."

Psychiatrist and psychical researcher Dr. Barthold Schwartz reported a somewhat different sort of ghostly phone event. He had interviewed a New Jersey woman called Marie.

One night Marie had a frightening dream about her old friend Lana. She saw Lana sinking into a pool of blood. The next day she phoned Lana—though they had not been in contact for quite a long time.

Lana sounded fine but admitted that she had been ill, and in the hospital. She said that she would be going back to the hospital the next day. Marie said that she would like to visit her friend in the hospital or at least call her. But Lana discouraged both suggestions, saying that she would call Marie as soon as she was better. It seemed a normal conversation.

Days passed and Lana did not call so Marie got worried. She called her home several times but no one answered. She finally got in touch with Lana's husband, who told her sadly that Lana was dead—that she had died six months ago, long before the phone conversation between Marie and Lana could possibly have taken place.

Was this a case of a phone call *to* a ghost?

The most famous phone-call-making ghost in America is named Rebecca. She haunts a large mountain inn called The Lodge in New Mexico. No one is really afraid of Rebecca; in fact, she's something of a tourist attraction. She's regularly written up in the local newspapers, and her story has even been featured on television. The restaurant in The Lodge is called Rebecca in her honor and portraits of her, even a stained-glass window, decorate The Lodge.

The portraits are entirely imaginary. No one knows what Rebecca looked like or who she was. According to the most popular story, she was a waitress at The Lodge during the 1930s. She was supposed to have been shot by her lumberjack lover when he found her with another man. No one is even sure where the name Rebecca came from. But it has stuck.

The ghost of Rebecca does all the traditional ghostly things. There are mysterious footsteps in the hall. Doors open, and close, as if by an unseen hand. Some employees have even claimed to have seen the apparition of an attractive red-haired woman in a long gown wandering the halls.

But Rebecca's most notable trait is that she likes to make phone calls. Usually she make her calls from

Suite 101, the Governor's Suite and the best room in the house. She doesn't seem to be calling anyone in particular. She just wants to let people know that she's still around.

Years ago The Lodge had an old-fashioned plug-in type of switchboard. An operator would sit at the board. When someone wanted to place a call from one of the rooms, a light would go on at the switchboard, and the operator would put a plug in a hole under the light to connect the call. The light for Room 101 kept going on, even if the room was not occupied. The switchboard was checked many times but nothing was mechanically wrong with it. It was as if some invisible figure in the room kept trying to make a call. Finally the operators would leave Room 101 plugged in all the time so they wouldn't be bothered.

The plug-in switchboard has long been replaced by a new electronic switchboard that is all automatic. That hasn't really changed Rebecca's behavior. The switchboard still keeps registering calls from Room 101, even when no one is in the room—no one alive, that is.

Often guests in Room 101 will find their phone ringing. When they pick it up no one is on the line, and when they ask the hotel operator why some joker keeps ringing their room and hanging up, they are told it's only Rebecca. Guests are not really scared. Actually, it's more of an honor.

2

A Hitch in Time

Maybe you think strange and ghostly events only happen at midnight. Or in spooky places like old castles, abandoned houses, and graveyards. Or involve a terrible event like a suicide or a murder. But that's not true. Sometimes the strangest things can happen in the most ordinary settings. That's what makes such events so frightening. They leave you with the feeling that in the middle of a perfectly normal, boring day, the most extraordinary thing can happen.

Take the case of Mrs. Coleen Buterbaugh of Lincoln, Nebraska. She never expected to see a ghost. She certainly didn't expect to see one on the morning of October 3, 1963. That morning Mrs. Buterbaugh went to work, as usual, at Nebraska Wesleyan University in Lincoln. She was a secretary in the office of Dean Sam Dahl. She was at work, as always, at eight in the morning. For the first forty-five minutes she did typing and other routine chores. There had been absolutely nothing out of the ordinary about the morning so far.

At about a quarter to nine Dean Dahl asked Mrs. Buterbaugh to carry a message to Dr. Tom McCourt who had an office in the nearby C.C. White Building. Dr. McCourt was a music teacher, and the White Building contained the offices of the music department. For a moment Mrs. Buterbaugh wondered why Dean Smith hadn't just picked up the phone and called Dr. McCourt. But that didn't matter much. It was just a short walk.

Mrs. Buterbaugh entered the White Building. The building looked as it always did. Some girls in the hall were going into class. She could hear someone practicing a musical instrument in one of the rooms along the hall. All perfectly ordinary, perfectly normal.

Mrs. Buterbaugh walked down the hall a short distance and entered the first of the two rooms that were occupied by Dr. McCourt. She went about four steps into the first room when she was suddenly hit by an almost overpowering odor. "I mean the kind that simply stops you in your tracks and almost chokes you," she said. It was musty and gave the impression that she was in a place that was very old, and had not been occupied for a long time.

Then she noticed something else. A moment earlier she had been surrounded by the normal sounds of a college building. Now there were no sounds at all. "Everything was deathly quiet."

For some reason Mrs. Buterbaugh found herself staring through the door to the second room of Dr. McCourt's suite, and at an old music cabinet that stood against the back wall of the room. There was an unfamiliar female figure in front of the cabinet. The figure was facing the cabinet, and thus had her back to Mrs. Buterbaugh. But Mrs. Buterbaugh could clearly see that the figure was that of an extremely tall and thin woman, wearing a long-sleeved white blouse and an ankle-length dark skirt. The woman's hair was piled on top of her head in a distinctly old-fashioned hairdo. The figure's arm was raised, as if reaching for something in the cabinet.

For several seconds the figure didn't move. But neither did Mrs. Buterbaugh. She didn't try to walk toward it, or call to it, or run away. She just stood there and stared. The figure looked completely real—it was not vague or transparent—yet somehow Mrs. Buterbaugh knew that it wasn't real. Quite suddenly the woman at the cabinet disappeared. She didn't fade out

or dissolve—she just disappeared, without having ever moved.

However, the experience wasn't over yet. Mrs. Buterbaugh got the distinct impression that there was someone else in the room with her, that a man was sitting at a desk on her left. She turned her head quickly. No one was there. But she still couldn't shake the strong feeling of another presence.

Mrs. Buterbaugh got her greatest shock when she looked through the window behind the desk. The window looked out on the University's Willard House, the girls' dormitory, and there was a street half a block away. Both were usually clearly visible through that window, but on this occasion she could see neither. All she could see were a few trees, in the rolling countryside. She also had the vague impression of a building on the right, but she could not see it clearly. Though this was an October morning, Mrs. Buterbaugh was sure that she was looking out on a warm summer afternoon scene. Everything was very still. "That was when I realized that these people were not in my time, but that I was back in their time."

That realization scared her. Mrs. Buterbaugh retreated from the room. Back out in the hallway the time returned to normal. The girls were still going into their class. The sound of a musical instrument being practiced nearby once again reached her ears.

Mrs. Buterbaugh forgot her original errand. She rushed back to her office in the Old Main Building. She wondered what to do next. If she told people what had happened they might think she was crazy. She tried to put the whole experience out of her mind—but she couldn't. After about half an hour she decided to tell Dean Dahl what had happened. The Dean did not think she was crazy; he knew her too well. He assumed that she was telling the truth.

The next step was to try and find out what had happened. Some of the older members of the faculty remembered that the two rooms in which Mrs. Buterbaugh's experience had taken place had been used for many years by a Miss Clara Urania Mills, a music teacher with a special interest in choral music. She had been at the University from 1912 until her death in 1936. The old-timers remembered Miss Mills as a very tall woman with black hair.

A picture of Miss Mills was found in a 1915 yearbook. Though Mrs. Buterbaugh had not seen the face of the apparition at the cabinet, she was convinced it was that of the tall music teacher. The figure she had seen was also tall and thin. Her hairstyle was the same as that in the yearbook photograph.

The cabinet drawer for which the figure seemed to have been reaching contained copies of old choral music—much of it dating from before 1936, the time

Clara Urania Mills, who was probably
the tall music teacher.

of Miss Mills's death. Since choral music was her chief
interest, the music in the cabinet may have been hers.

The 1915 yearbook also contained photos of the
campus. It looked like the scene Mrs. Buterbaugh had
observed through the window during that brief but
frightening moment. She had never seen old pictures
of the campus before.

The case came to the attention of the American
Society for Psychical Research—which is always in-

terested in strange and ghostly events. Dr. Gardner Murphy, the president of the society, thought it was so interesting that he personally went out to Nebraska to investigate.

He didn't think that Mrs. Buterbaugh was lying, or crazy. He believed that she had seen and experienced "something." Just what had happened, and why it happened at that particular moment, remained a mystery.

What puzzled Dr. Murphy and others is why this particular scene—Miss Mills reaching into the music cabinet—should have been presented at all. Miss Mills had died at the school, at about 9:00 in the morning. That was roughly the same time of day Mrs. Buterbaugh had her experience. But Miss Mills had died in a room across the hall, not in the room where she was "seen." Her death had taken place in midwinter, and the scene presented was that of midsummer. Besides, the clothes were of a much earlier era, about 1915, not 1936, the year of Miss Mills's death.

In many accounts of ghosts there is the motive of a search, an attempt by the ghost to find something important here on earth, a treasure or a lost will, for example. In other accounts the ghost returns to take care of some vital unfinished business, like identifying his or her murderer. This apparition appears to have been looking for choral music. That search seems so trivial to most of us that it's almost funny. But Miss Mills was a woman who was devoted to choral music—

so perhaps the search was important to her!

So you never know when these things may jump out at you. You don't have to be in a haunted house, or a graveyard. You may just be walking along the corridor of your school, seeing the ordinary sights, listening to the ordinary sounds, when all of a sudden . . .

3

"Beware!—Jack"

The spirits are supposed to communicate with the living in a variety of ways. As we have just seen, in recent years they have even been making phone calls. Sometimes the spirits are supposed to take charge of the body of a particularly sensitive person called a medium, and speak through him or her. At other times the spirits are said to direct the action of some sort of a device, like a Ouija board.

But, historically speaking, the most popular form of spiritual communication is automatic writing. That's when the spirits are supposed to take control of a person's hand—or if the person happens to be using a typewriter, both hands—and direct the writing. The human subject—the person who is actually doing the writing—has no conscious control over what is being written.

There are a lot of people who have claimed to produce whole books by automatic writing. If that is what's actually happening, then the spirits are a wordy and boring bunch. Earlier in this century a St. Louis housewife named Pearl Curran claimed that she was writing under the direction of a spirit named Patience Worth. Patience Worth (or Pearl Curran) produced an astonishing flow of poems and stories and novels—millions of words. For a while Patience Worth had a following—but no one reads the stuff today, for good reason; it's very dull.

But every once in a while there is a case involving automatic writing that is a good deal more exciting. Take, for example, what happened in the vacation village of Pentwater, Michigan, in the early 1960s.

At one time Pentwater was a very elegant place. The summer homes built there by rich people were practically mansions. By the 1960s that opulent style of summer life, when wealthy families had lots of servants, had practically disappeared.

However, some of the big old summer houses were still occupied. One of them was the home of Celeste McVoy Holden. This summer was a lonely time for Celeste. She had just separated from her husband,

Jack. A couple of servants came during the day, but they lived in town, and she was alone with her four-month-old baby all night.

Celeste had asked her friend, Buell Mullen, to spend a few weeks with her at the house, and Buell agreed. Buell's husband had some business to take care of and was not able to come out to the summer house at once. He had arranged to join the two women at Pentwater later in the week.

Shortly after Buell arrived at the house she sat down to write her husband a letter. It contained the rather complicated directions needed for getting to the Holden house, which was in an isolated spot well back in the woods.

As Buell was writing it seemed to her that suddenly some invisible force took control of her hand. She struggled to get control back, but without success. Buell watched with fascination and horror as her own hand began to write a message. The handwriting was quite different from her own. So were the thoughts. The message read:

"Beware! Beware! Beware!"

Buell had no idea what this meant. Then her hand scrawled a final word: "Jack." After that the force released her hand.

Badly shaken, Buell took the message and showed it to Celeste. The words had a great impact on her, for Jack was the name of her ex-husband. Celeste had divorced him largely because of his violent and uncontrollable temper. During and after the divorce Jack had been extremely bitter and she often worried that he might do something violent, though he had never made any threats. Was it possible that he was now planning something, and that this message was a warning?

The two women thought that if they used a Ouija board they might be able to get more information about the warning. They didn't have one in the house but were able to buy one in Pentwater.

The message delivered via the Ouija board was even more terrifying than the one that had come via automatic writing. When Celeste asked what was going to happen, the board quickly spelled out: "Murder, you and your child." The board's final word was: "Prepare!"

What could they do? Call the police and tell them that a message on a Ouija board had warned them about murder that might be committed? The police certainly wouldn't believe that story. The women had no guns or other weapons in the house.

All they could do was move into the most secure part of the house and make doubly sure that all the doors and windows were locked. The two women didn't get any sleep that night. They stayed up playing cards, and jumping every time they heard a sound.

Finally, dawn came. Nothing had happened. Celeste and Buell were tired and relieved. But they also

felt just a bit foolish. Had all this excitement been for nothing?

Two days later they discovered that they had not been foolish after all. A friend called and asked Celeste if she had seen her ex-husband recently. She said no, that she didn't even think he was in the area anymore.

The friend then told her that just two nights earlier—the night the women had received the warning and hidden in the locked room—Jack had showed up at a party in a nearby town. He was very drunk, and he had a gun. He began waving the gun around and saying that he was going to kill his ex-wife and child.

Some of the men at the party grabbed Jack and took the gun away from him. They held him until he sobered up a bit and calmed down. By three in the morning he seemed to have come back to his senses, and he was allowed to leave. No one had seen him since.

Had Jack really left town, as he promised the people at the party he would? Or did he go down to the old house still intent on carrying out his death threat? Perhaps he became discouraged when he discovered that the woman he hated had barricaded herself in the house. Whatever the truth, it's clear enough that the threat was real when the warnings came through.

4

The Airline Ghosts

Ghosts are often said to linger around the place where they died. Sometimes that habit takes a curious twist. Take, for example, the ghosts that are associated with Eastern Airlines Flight 401.

On the night of Friday, December 29, 1972, Eastern Airlines Flight 401 from New York to Miami was approaching Miami International Airport. In the cockpit a warning light alerted the crew that something was wrong with the nose landing gear. The pilot of Flight 401, Captain Bob Loft, radioed the tower at Miami that their landing would be delayed. The plane made a wide circle as the crew tried to correct the problem, and apparently did so. But as Flight 401 came around for a second attempt at a landing, it was much too close to the ground. As a result the plane crashed into the shallow waters of the Florida Everglades, a few miles from the airport.

The crash was witnessed by people on the ground, and by other planes that were either arriving or departing from the Miami airport. As far as the air traffic controllers at the airport were concerned, Flight 401 had simply disappeared from their radar screens.

If there is such a thing as a soft airplane crash, that is what Flight 401 experienced. The crew apparently was aware of what was about to happen, and did everything possible to cushion the impact. The plane crashed in shallow water and didn't break up completely. The water also helped douse any fires. Since the crash was well witnessed, and close to a major city, help could and did arrive quickly. As a result of this fortunate combination of circumstances there were survivors of the crash—some seventy of them. But there were more victims than survivors. One hundred and one passengers and crew members died in the crash of Flight 401.

Of course, there was an investigation. As usual, it wasn't possible to determine exactly what had happened, since the pilot and others responsible for the operation of the plane had been in the cockpit when the crash occurred and had been killed. The best ex-

A man is dwarfed by remains of rear jet engine and tail assembly of L-1011 after it crashed in the Everglades.

planation investigators could come up with was a combination of faulty equipment and pilot error. Either the nose landing gear had actually failed to lower properly, or a faulty warning light told the crew that it had failed. In any case, they were so distracted trying to correct this error that they failed to keep track of the plane's altitude. By the time they realized just how close to the ground they were, it was too late.

The plane that had crashed was an L-1011 jumbo jet, a very popular type of aircraft. There were lots of L-1011s flying for Eastern and other airlines.

Just as there had been human survivors of the crash

of Flight 401, large portions of the plane itself survived without serious damage. After the investigations the parts of the L-1011 that had been Flight 401 and that were still in working order were used as spare parts for other L-1011s in Eastern's fleet. Just as parts of a wrecked car may be used to repair other cars, it's the same with airplanes. In fact, it's even more common with airplanes, since parts for them are a lot more expensive.

Within a few months after the crash strange rumors began to circulate among Eastern Airlines employees. The ghosts of Captain Bob Loft and Flight Engineer Don Repo, who had been killed in the crash of Flight 401, were being seen on other Eastern flights. The reports came mainly from an L-1011 with the number 318, a plane almost identical to the one that had crashed in the Everglades in December, 1972. Many of those who saw the apparitions had known the dead men before the crash, so were quick to recognize them.

The airline employees didn't want to talk publicly about their experiences. They were afraid that people would think they were crazy, and they might lose their jobs. Who wants to fly on an airplane with a crazy crew? The airline didn't want to talk about the rumors either. Who wants to fly on a haunted airplane? But the airline employees talked to one another. And they told the stories to their friends and relatives. So rumors of the ghosts got around. Eventually the rumors were

Captain Robert
A. Loft

Flight Engineer
Don Repo

heard by a writer named John Fuller. He set out to investigate. At first people wouldn't talk to him, but eventually they loosened up, and he collected some pretty astonishing accounts.

On one flight the flight engineer was going through his routine preflight inspection. He saw a man wearing the uniform of an Eastern Airlines flight engineer sitting in his seat. He recognized the man as the now dead Don Repo. The apparition of Repo said something like, "You don't need to worry about the preflight. I've already done it." Immediately after that the figure vanished.

One flight was actually canceled after the pilot and two flight attendants encountered the ghost of Captain Loft in the first-class compartment.

In another incident the flight attendant was making a final headcount of the passengers. She counted one extra in first class. She figured it was the fellow in the Eastern Airlines uniform. Airline employees are often able to ride free if seats are available, but they do need a special boarding pass and most check in. The flight attendant tried to talk to the man, but he stared straight ahead and didn't answer. She called the pilot. He came to look at the silent man and shouted, "My God, it's Bob Loft." Then the figure vanished.

During a flight on an L-1011 one of the flight attendants discovered that an oven used for heating meals had an overloaded circuit. A man in an engineer's uniform appeared and fixed the oven. A few minutes later another engineer showed up, and when he was told that the oven had already been fixed, he insisted that he was the only engineer on the flight. Later the flight attendant identified a photo of Don Repo as the man who had fixed the oven.

On a plane approaching Miami International Airport, over the Everglades, the same path taken by the ill-fated Flight 401, a voice came over the PA system to announce the usual seat belt and no smoking rules to passengers and crew. No one in the regular crew made the announcement; in fact, the PA system wasn't even turned on during that period!

These are just a few of the dozens of accounts that Fuller collected for his book, *The Ghost of Flight 401*. Fuller felt that the majority of the encounters with the ghosts of Captain Loft or Don Repo had occurred on one particular plane, #318, because that plane used a large number of salvaged parts from the crashed plane. Other L-1011s on which there had also been sightings of the ghosts had also used parts from the Flight 401 plane.

Though those who saw the figures of Captain Loft or Flight Engineer Repo were usually quite shaken, the ghosts themselves do not seem to have been at all menacing. In fact, they seemed to want to be helpful in a small way, like fixing an oven, or making an announcement about fastening seat belts. Still, the airline employees wished that they would go away. Even a helpful ghost can be very unsettling.

Finally, some of the people who had seen the apparitions felt that they were able to get in touch with the spirit of Don Repo through use of a Ouija board.

Eventually the number of sightings dwindled and faded away.

5
Something
in the Room

Ancient castles and grand manor houses in England often have a "haunted room." That's the bedroom where they never put guests because some ancestor or other was murdered there, and his ghost continues to haunt the room and disturb the sleep of the guests. Guests who spend a night in the haunted room sometimes die of fright or go mad. At the very least they flee the castle the next morning, never to return.

That's fine for castles, but certainly one does not expect to find a horribly haunted room in a small frame house, not in Detroit, and not in 1961. Yet that's just what auto worker Bill Cole and his family found—to their horror.

Bill purchased the house partly because it had a small back bedroom. He was employed at the Cadillac assembly plant, and he often worked the night shift. That meant he came home in the morning and had to sleep during the day. The Coles had three active and noisy children, so Bill was finding it pretty hard to sleep during the day in their old house.

The new house, a gray frame building on Martin Street, had this small back bedroom. It was isolated from the rest of the house. The room looked as if it had been added to the house after the original structure was built. It was so small that you could just about squeeze a single bed into it. It also had a tiny closet, but with a bed in the room you couldn't even open the closet door completely. The only way to get into the room was through a door from the kitchen—not very convenient—but Bill thought it would be perfect for his needs. No one would bother him back there.

The first week in his new house Bill tried the room out. He came home in the morning from his work on the night shift. He went to the little bedroom, climbed into bed and promptly fell asleep. A few minutes later he was in the grip of the worst, and most lifelike nightmare he had ever experienced. In his dream he had walked over to the closet door, opened it slowly and looked in. Inside was a bloody and horribly mutilated corpse propped up against the wall. Bill woke up covered with sweat and his heart was pounding wildly.

Bill tried to pass the whole thing off as the result of the excitement of moving, and the disruptions of his irregular work schedule. Still it took him a few minutes to get the courage to actually check the closet. It was empty. He found it difficult to get back to sleep again.

The horrifying dream recurred every time Bill went to sleep in the back bedroom. He was now so tired that his work at the auto plant was suffering. He finally just gave up trying to sleep in the room. He went back to sleeping in the main bedroom. There his sleep was untroubled. He didn't go into any details about why he didn't go into the little room anymore. He just told his wife, Lillian, that he didn't feel comfortable there.

Bill soon became completely adjusted to sleeping in the main bedroom during the day. The sounds of his children playing, or other daytime noises didn't bother him anymore. And the memory of those horrible dreams that he had when sleeping in the back bedroom began to fade. After all, everything else about this house seemed perfectly ordinary and normal. Bill pushed the whole experience to the back of his mind. He treated it as some sort of odd, but temporary, event. He figured it was all over.

In late summer of 1962 Bill's mother came for a visit. Bill's wife suggested that she sleep in the little back bedroom, rather than on a couch in the living room. Lillian pointed out that they had a perfectly good empty room. Why have Grandma Cole sleep on the couch? Bill was a bit uneasy, but he told himself that the bad dreams were his problem, and had nothing to do with the room.

Two days later Grandma Cole cut short her visit and was on her way back to Georgia. She didn't have nightmares, but said she was kept awake by a thumping sound coming from the closet. It filled her with a feeling of dread, and she was convinced that something was in the closet hammering on the door, trying to get out. She also felt that if she opened the closet door, it—whatever it was—would "get" her. No one else heard the thumping. Looking in the closet and seeing it was empty did little to calm her fears. She knew what she heard and felt. Not only wouldn't she stay in the room, she didn't even want to stay in the house anymore.

For the first time Bill sat down and told his wife what he had experienced. Lillian admitted that she too often felt uncomfortable when she went in to clean the room, and she did so as rarely as possible. They noticed that their dog, normally an extremely brave little terrier, avoided the room. So did the children, who usually got into everything. When asked, the children could not be sure why they didn't go into the back bedroom. It was just a feeling they had. They didn't like it.

Bill locked the door to the room, and decided never to use it again. But he also felt a bit foolish giving in to these "superstitious" fears. In October, 1962, Bill's old friend Dick Patterson visited the Cole house. Patterson was the calmest, most level-headed person that the Coles knew. So they decided to put him in the back bedroom. But they didn't tell him about what had happened to others. They didn't want him to be influenced.

Patterson went to bed at about 11:00 P.M. Sometime shortly after midnight he woke up. He felt someone was trying to shake him or turn him over. The bedroom door, which led to the kitchen, was open. He distinctly remembered having closed it before he went to bed. In the doorway was the figure of a woman. She had her back turned to Patterson and was apparently staring out into the kitchen. At first Patterson assumed that the figure was Lillian Cole. But the hair was different, and the woman was wearing what appeared to be a long blue dress and a short fur coat—not the sort of clothes he had ever seen Lillian wear.

Patterson got out of bed and walked toward the figure, but before he reached it all the lights in the house went out. A few seconds later they went on again. Patterson was in the kitchen. Lillian was there; she was washing her hair in the sink. The mysterious figure in the doorway had disappeared.

Patterson tried to explain to Lillian what had happened, but she didn't need an explanation. She confessed to Patterson that a lot of strange things had already happened in that back bedroom.

As the two stood talking in the kitchen they heard strange and awful howling noises coming from the back bedroom. Then came a choking smell—the smell of rotting flesh—that made both of them sick. The most frightening thing of all was that a trapdoor to the cellar that was located in a utility room off the kitchen began to rise slowly, and then suddenly slammed shut.

Lillian grabbed the phone and called the police. When the police arrived they were suspicious. They thought someone might be playing a joke on them. But they were impressed by Lillian's and Patterson's obvious sincerity, and equally obvious fear. The police carefully searched the whole house, including the back bedroom and the cellar. They found nothing out of the ordinary.

When Bill came home from work the next morning he found his wife and friend still sitting in the kitchen discussing what had happened that night. Bill was thoroughly ashamed of himself. He had put his mother in the haunted room. Then he put his friend there. Now he was determined to settle the matter once and for all. He was going to go back into that room and spend the night.

Since he wasn't scheduled to work for two days, he waited until evening to go into the room. He figured that since he was very tired he would sleep straight through, if nothing happened.

He got into bed that evening, and despite all his previous troubles sleeping in the room, he dropped

right off. After about an hour he was awakened by a noise in the room. In the semidarkness he saw the shape of a woman standing near the door. He thought it was Lillian and he called loudly to her. The figure turned. It wasn't Lillian; it wasn't even human anymore. Whatever it was had the face of a rotting corpse. The figure moved toward him, and held its face just a few inches from his own. It appeared to be trying to speak, but all that came out were hissing sounds.

Bill jumped out of bed, and somehow in the narrow confines of that tiny room he managed to get past the hideous figure without touching it, and run into the kitchen. He was hysterical. Patterson and Lillian had to throw a blanket around him to keep him from rushing out into the street and possibly hurting himself.

No one else in the house saw the terrible figure. It's possible that Bill just had another of those realistic dreams. It's possible that all of the other things that were supposed to have happened in that house could have natural explanations. Bill Cole no longer cared. The very next day the family packed up and moved in with Lillian's parents in the suburbs.

The frame house was put up for sale. The real estate agent never told prospective buyers why the last family had moved out so abruptly, and no one else who has lived there has ever experienced any of the strange and terrible phenomena that afflicted the Coles.

6

"My Hands Are Free from Blood"

The annals of ghost lore are filled with tales of persons who returned from the dead to right some wrong that had been done to them. That certainly seemed to be the motive of the ghost of Lt. James Sutton.

Sutton was a lieutenant at the Naval Academy at Annapolis, Maryland. On the night of October 12, 1907, according to the official report, Lieutenant Sutton had attended a dance, where he had quite a bit to drink. During his trip back to Annapolis with some of his buddies, a fight broke out. In the fight Sutton was thrown to the ground. After the incident he seemed to go berserk. He shouted and threatened to kill the other men with him. When he got back to camp he went directly to his tent where he grabbed two pistols. However, he was spotted carrying the weapons, stopped, questioned, and told he was going to be arrested.

Before Lieutenant Sutton could be disarmed he began shooting wildly. No one was hit. But as the other Navy men watched in horror, Lieutenant Sutton very deliberately put a pistol to his own head and pulled the trigger. The time was 1:30 A.M. of the morning of the 13th of October.

The official explanation was that Lt. James Sutton had killed himself while in the grip of some sort of insane, drunken rage.

Lieutenant Sutton's family lived all the way across the country in Portland, Oregon. He had written a letter home that arrived on October 13, the day he died. In the letter Lieutenant Sutton complained of being a bit homesick, but on the whole sounded cheerful, and not at all like someone who was about to kill himself. But despite the tone of the letter, his mother felt something was wrong. She was nervous all day.

It wasn't until the evening of October 13th that a telegram arrived to inform the Sutton family of their son's death. As soon as Mrs. Sutton was told what had happened, she had a vision of her son standing in front of her.

"At that instant," she said, "Jimmie stood right before me and said, 'Mama, I never killed myself . . . my hands are free from blood as when I was five years old.' "

No one else in the room saw the figure of the dead man. You might think that Mrs. Sutton was having a reaction because of the shock and grief she felt. And that's what everyone would have thought if the story ended there. But it didn't.

The apparition of Lt. James Sutton kept on appearing to his mother. And he began to provide details of his own death.

". . . a man hit me on the head with the butt of a gun so that I fell on my knees; then three of them jumped me and beat me . . . They broke my watch with a kick as I lay on the ground."

On the 15th of October Jimmie's sister, Daisy, had a dream. She was in her room. "I saw an arm holding a photograph before me. I got the impression of someone saying to me, 'There is the picture of the man who was most interested in directing the fight that killed Jimmie.' "

A few days later while looking through some of her brother's belongings, she saw a picture of a group of young officers and student officers. Jimmie Sutton was one of the group. His sister also recognized "at the lower right corner the face I had seen on the photograph in my dream, if it was a dream." The name of the officer was Lieutenant Utley.

A few weeks after his death, Lieutenant Sutton's

parents claimed his clothes and the personal items that he had with him at the time of his death. They felt these confirmed what the apparition of the young man had been saying. The clothes he had worn on his last day seemed to indicate that he had received a beating. His watch was broken just as the apparition had said.

The Suttons felt that the story they had been told by the Navy simply didn't make sense. They could find no reason why the fight started in the first place. Nor could they see any particular reason why James Sutton, whom they felt was neither a violent boy nor a heavy drinker, would suddenly have gone into a rage and killed himself. The testimonies of those who were on the scene did not match. And finally, the authorities who had investigated the case never even considered the possibility that Lieutenant Sutton had been killed, rather than killed himself. It seemed as if they had their minds made up before any investigation.

For almost two years the apparition of her dead son continued to appear to Mrs. Sutton, urging her to clear his name. And for all that time the Sutton family continued to pester the government for more information, for more investigation.

Finally, in 1909, the body, which had been buried in Arlington Cemetery, was exhumed. After all that time the remains were badly decomposed. But an examination did show that the lieutenant had been badly beaten before he died. When he first died Navy doctors insisted that he had not been beaten. All along, the ghost insisted that he had. It turned out the ghost was right.

The autopsy also suggested that the angle of the bullet and the nature of the wound were not consistent with the theory that Lieutenant Sutton shot himself.

When the witnesses to Lieutenant Sutton's death were questioned again it turned out that none of them actually saw the young man shoot himself. They simply assumed, or said, that's what he did.

And that is just about where the story ends. No final proof of the fate of Lieutenant Sutton could ever be offered. The official verdict of suicide was never changed. Nothing was ever uncovered to tie the mysterious Lieutenant Utley to the death. But the Sutton family felt they had been vindicated.

So apparently did the dead man. His apparition appeared less and less frequently to his mother. Finally, it disappeared altogether.

The case itself remains unsolved.

7

Pipe Smoke

You probably think of ghosts as being frightening. Most people do. But as often as not, those who report actually seeing a ghost say that the ghost did not appear to terrify or harm people. Quite the opposite. The ghost appeared to help the living.

That is certainly the case with the ghost that appeared to Mrs. Elaine Worrell.

The place was the town of Oskaloosa, Iowa. The year was 1949. World War II had not been over for very long. The war had created a tremendous housing shortage. There were no houses to buy and few apartments to rent.

After some searching, Elaine Worrell and her husband, Hal, found an apartment. It was in a large old house in Oskaloosa that had been renovated into tiny apartments. The apartments were so small that they didn't have their own bathrooms. The residents of each floor shared a single bathroom in the hall.

The Worrells had an apartment on the top floor. There was only one other apartment on that floor. It was occupied by a young widow named Patricia Burns.

The landlady told the Worrells that Patricia Burns's story was a tragic one. Her husband had been killed in an industrial accident a few months earlier. She had moved to Oskaloosa to try to start a new life. But she had really been unable to recover from the grief. Patricia still spent most of her days in her tiny apartment, playing the piano. She was an excellent pianist.

In the months that the Worrells lived in the Oskaloosa apartment they saw little of their neighbor. From time to time Elaine would pass the young widow in the hall. They would exchange polite greetings, but that was all. Elaine had no wish to impose herself on her neighbor. For her part Patricia did not appear to want to hold long conversations with anyone.

The arrangement did not make Elaine Worrell unduly uncomfortable. People who live in cramped quarters learn to block others out of their lives in order to maintain some privacy.

Hal Worrell often had to work weekends. Elaine

didn't like being stuck alone in a small apartment for the weekend, but they needed the money. She had become quite reconciled to Hal's weekend work. One Saturday, though, Elaine began to feel very uneasy and uncomfortable about being left alone. She couldn't think of any particular reason why she should feel so jumpy, but she did. She thought that a warm bath might relax her, though she didn't usually take baths in the middle of the day. Elaine put on her robe, and walked down the hall to the bathroom. The room was dark, and she felt around for the light cord. It was then that she noticed that the air was filled with the smoke from a sweet and aromatic pipe tobacco.

As the light went on Elaine turned quickly toward the doorway. A young man was standing there. She had not passed him in the hall, and had no idea where he had come from. The young man had curly black hair and there was a small scar on his left cheekbone. The smoke came from a pipe that he held in his hand. Elaine had never seen this young man before.

She should have been frightened by the sudden appearance of the stranger, but somehow she wasn't. And she wasn't sure he was really there. She looked into his eyes and realized that he never blinked. He didn't seem to see her at all. It was as if he was in some other world.

The figure turned and walked down the hall toward Patricia Burns's apartment. Elaine followed. She didn't

want to follow but it was as if she was pushed by some unknown force. When the apparition reached the door of the widow's apartment it hesitated for a moment, and then it vanished.

Elaine knew what she had to do next. The figure had been there for a purpose—to bring her to Patricia Burns's door. But why? She knocked softly. There was no answer. She knocked a little louder, still no answer. Finally, she tried the apartment door. It was unlocked.

Tentatively she entered the apartment, calling out, "Mrs. Burns, Mrs. Burns, are you there, are you all right?" There was no answer.

She found the widow on the bedroom floor, covered with blood. Patricia Burns had slashed her wrists, and was now unconscious and near death from the loss of blood.

Fortunately Elaine knew first aid. She tore up a bed sheet in order to make tourniquets to stop the bleeding. She then called her husband at work. He knew where to find a doctor. A few minutes later Hal and the doctor arrived. The doctor took care of the wounds. They were not deep, but if Elaine had not arrived when she did, the young woman would certainly have died.

As is so often the case in suicide attempts, Patricia Burns was extremely grateful that someone had arrived in time to save her life. The next day she told Elaine that she had been exceptionally depressed in the few days before she tried to kill herself. She had also started drinking. Almost overcome by despair, she decided to join her husband in death by slashing her wrists.

Patricia did not ask why Elaine had come to the door at the exact moment she did. And Elaine said nothing about the figure she had seen. But she did realize that the figure must have appeared at almost the exact moment when Patricia attempted to take her own life.

As the women talked, Patricia began to reminisce about her dead husband, Raymond. It was the first time Elaine had ever heard the man's name. From a drawer Patricia drew a framed picture. It showed a smiling Patricia Burns standing next to a young man with curly dark hair, a small scar on his left cheekbone, and cradling a pipe in his hand. A shiver went through Elaine. It was the same man she had seen in the bathroom door, the same man who had led her to the door of the apartment and to her life-saving discovery. Somehow, Raymond Burns had known of his wife's danger, and was still able to bring help.

8

Massey's Mice
of Death

Danton Walker was a New York newspaper columnist. He wrote a gossip column about the entertainment and night life scene. During the 1940s and 1950s, when his column was most popular, he knew all the Broadway celebrities.

Walker had another interest, the supernatural. He just loved to collect ghost stories or other spooky tales. He particularly loved these tales if they were about some of the famous people he knew. There is probably no one who knew more celebrity ghost stories than Danton Walker.

One of the most unusual stories he collected was

from Dorothy Massey, wife of the actor Raymond Massey.

Early in the 1940s the Masseys decided that they were going to buy a house in New York City. They looked at a block where a number of houses were available. Today it is almost impossible to buy a house in Manhattan. In the early 1940s there were lots of houses for sale.

Dorothy fell in love with the first house they looked at. Somehow Ray didn't like it. He couldn't exactly explain what it was about the house he didn't like. He just felt he wouldn't be comfortable there. It was an emotional reaction, a hunch.

So the Masseys kept on looking and finally bought the house across the street. This house wasn't as nice, and it was more expensive, but the actor felt comfortable there. Dorothy Massey had long ago learned it was useless to argue with her husband's hunches. She thought the first house was better, but was quite satisfied with the house they got.

The Masseys settled themselves into their new home quickly enough. A few months later Dorothy met the woman who bought the house across the street—the one the Masseys had first considered. The woman thought it was a wonderful house, and had been a great bargain, but . . .

"There's one thing about it that bothers me: we have mice. We have tried practically everything to get rid of them but they just refuse to get out. They seem to be even more attached to the place than we are!"

A few months later Dorothy was idly looking out of the window of her house at the house across the street. She saw a crowd of mice come running out of the basement.

"They came out in groups, in a panicky sort of way, confused and scurrying along the gutter. Then one or two got brave and made the bold dash across the street to my house. I immediately ran to the phone to call the exterminator."

All attempts to get rid of the mice failed, until the Masseys got a couple of cats. The cats kept the mouse population under control, though there were still plenty in the house. It was not the mice themselves, but their behavior, that is the point of this story.

A couple of days after the mouse migration, Raymond Massey showed his wife a newspaper article about the suicide of a wealthy and socially prominent woman. It was the woman who lived across the street. She had died three days after the mice in her house had fled. Did the mice somehow sense what was coming?

Dorothy Massey dismissed the affair as a pure coincidence. Then it happened again. The family of the woman who had died moved out, and put the house on the market. The next buyer was a wealthy businessman, with a notorious reputation. He was always

getting married and divorced. He also had a lot of girl friends. One of them moved into the house.

A few months later the businessman died, apparently from natural causes. "Just before his death made front-page news, those darned mice moved out again." said Dorothy Massey. "I happened to be standing at the front window . . . when I saw it happen."

By now Dorothy was beginning to get a bit nervous. But the house remained vacant for a long time. So she pushed all thoughts of the migrating mice to the back of her mind. Eventually the house was sold again. Dorothy didn't know anything about the new owner. Other people on the street said that he was some sort of businessman. He seemed to be a very solid-citizen type, not the sort anyone expects to die suddenly. So Dorothy was quite unprepared for the sight of another mouse migration.

"I was watering some plants in the window box when I saw the little creatures going through the same rigmarole, and I went cold all over. What was going to happen now?"

It didn't take long for her to find out. A few days later she was sitting at breakfast with her husband, reading the *New York Times*. There was an item on the front page about a businessman who was returning from a trip to Canada in his own private plane. Somewhere over the Hudson River the plane went down. The businessman drowned before rescuers could reach him. Neither Dorothy nor Ray knew the man by name. But they certainly recognized his address. It was the address of the house across the street.

Then something even more unsettling happened. The mice that had been living in the basement of the Massey house began moving out, and heading for the house across the street. Was this an omen of death for the Masseys?

Nothing really terrible happened to the Massey family. The furnace blew up, but no one was hurt. And they were fully insured. Perhaps the mice knew what was coming, and since they lived in the basement, wanted to get away for their own sakes.

Still, after that the Masseys never felt comfortable in their house. When the chance came to buy a place in Connecticut, they jumped at it. They sold their house in New York and didn't even want to know the name of the new owner.

9

"I'll Never Leave You"

Reuben Weisberger ran a small grocery store on St. Clair Street in Cleveland during the 1850s and '60s. All in all, his customers and friends thought of him as a good man. He was honest and hard-working, even if he was a little overbearing. When he died, after a short illness, people in his Cleveland neighborhood were genuinely saddened.

Reuben had always been an excellent family man. He was extremely faithful to his wife, and shortly before his death he had promised, "I'll never leave you." Rosa Weisberger didn't take the promise seriously. Perhaps she should have.

Outwardly Rosa seemed to be very strong and courageous after her husband died. With help from her children she continued to run the grocery store. She didn't complain. She just kept right on working.

That was all a brave front—a show. Inside, Rosa was grief-stricken and felt completely lost. Reuben had been her entire life. She couldn't sleep. She ate very little and began losing weight. She became obsessed with the idea she had not said good-bye to him properly. She came to feel that if she could just see Reuben one more time, to say good-bye properly, then perhaps she could stop grieving over his death, and put her own life back together.

At that time a lot of people went to spirit mediums. The mediums were supposed to help them contact loved ones who had died. Rosa Weisberger didn't believe in spirit mediums, and she didn't disbelieve in them. She had never thought too much about the subject—until now. One of the customers mentioned a spirit medium named Silvie Heitman, who lived in the neighborhood. Rosa asked other customers about the medium. A lot of them had gone to see her after one of their loved ones died. The medium had an excellent reputation.

On the evening of July 13, 1870, Rosa visited Silvie Heitman, the medium. It was not at all as Rosa had expected. The medium was a plain, homey-looking woman like herself. There was nothing spooky or strange about her house. It looked very much like Rosa's own house. The two women got on well together, and talked pleasantly over several cups of coffee. Then Rosa made the request to see her dead husband one more time. The medium said she would try—but naturally could guarantee no results.

Silvie leaned back in her chair and went into a trance. Rosa watched as a pale glow, which did not seem to come from any particular source, filled the room. Suddenly there stood Reuben Weisberger, wearing his long grocer's apron, and looking just as he always had in life.

The apparition didn't move and didn't speak. But it was so real that Rosa nearly collapsed in horror. She had *asked* to see her dead husband. But she had not really *expected* to see him.

After the figure of the grocer vanished, Rosa was too shaken to go home alone. She asked Silvie if she could spend the night. The medium naturally agreed.

Early that morning the medium was awakened by a noise. She opened her eyes to find the room bathed in the same gray light that had accompanied the apparition of Reuben Weisberger. She looked toward the bed in which Rosa had been sleeping. It was empty.

The grocer's widow was at the far end of the room. She was getting dressed. Her movements, however, were jerky and mechanical, as though she were not in control of her own body. Silvie called to her, but

Rosa did not answer. She did not even seem to hear. The medium, who had spent so much of her life in close contact with the supernatural, was frightened by what she saw.

The mysterious gray light went out, and Silvie heard the door close as Rosa left the house.

Later that morning Silvie went to the Weisberger house. Rosa was there, and she had a strange story to tell. She said that she had no idea how or why she had left Silvie's house. All she knew is that she suddenly found herself in the home of her late husband's elderly mother. The old woman, who had always enjoyed excellent health, had been taken suddenly and seriously ill.

The medium said that the spirit of Reuben had returned again, and guided his wife to the bedside of his ailing mother. Rosa said she didn't believe it. But she was clearly nervous.

The medium came to visit Rosa once again that evening. She suggested that they take a walk, because it was a cool and pleasant night.

The two women had walked only a short distance when Rosa looked back and cried, "There he is." She grabbed the medium's arm. "Do you see him?"

The medium admitted that she did see the figure of Reuben behind them. "He's been following us the whole way," she said.

Now terrified, Rosa insisted on going home. But the

apparition had preceded them. It was in the house tossing plates and cups, and even chairs, about. The experience was more than poor Rosa could bear. She fainted, and after she awoke she was never the same again.

She complained that her dead husband followed her everywhere. She would often be seen on St. Clair Street mumbling to herself, and occasionally stopping to scream at Reuben's ghost that she insisted tagged along behind her. But no one else could see the spirit.

The people in the neighborhood would look at her and sadly shake their heads. "There goes poor Rosa," they would say to one another. "She's been out of her head since her husband died, poor thing."

They didn't know that the grocer had kept his promise of "I'll never leave you" all too well.

"Marche!"

Augustus Richard Peers was one of those hardy adventurers who is willing to endure the dangers and hardships of frontier life. In the 1840s Peers went to the far northern reaches of Canada to make his living as a fur trader.

For about three years he worked for the Hudson's Bay Company in their headquarters at Fort Simpson. He was then transferred farther north to a place called Fort Norman. Finally he was made manager of the company headquarters at Fort McPherson. Fort McPherson was the Hudson's Bay Company's most northerly outpost and as remote a spot as any on earth.

Life was not easy in the far northern outposts of the Hudson's Bay Company.

It was less than a hundred miles from the Arctic Ocean.

Peers was good at his work. He was well respected by the Hudson's Bay Company and well liked by the other fur traders and the Eskimos of the region.

He even managed to marry—no easy feat, for there were few women who wished to share the hardships and dangers of life in that bleak outpost and terrible climate. The Peers had two children, and they seemed happy. In truth, however, only Mrs. Peers was happy. For some reason, Peers himself had come to hate Fort McPherson. But just how much he hated it was not fully known until years after his death.

In the months before he died Augustus Peers had

become obsessed by feeling that he was about to die—though he was a relatively young man and not at all ill at the time. Still, he talked about his death constantly. He also told his wife, and everybody else who would listen, that he hated Fort McPherson and did not under any circumstances wish to be buried there. He also indicated that he hated his previous residence, Fort Norman, as well.

Peers died suddenly, and unexpectedly (unexpected by everyone but Peers himself), on March 15, 1853. Contrary to his wishes, he was buried at Fort McPherson. Burying the body at Fort McPherson was not just a case of callous disregard for a dead man's wish. Moving a corpse a long distance by dog sled—the only means of transportation available—was no easy task. It was not to be undertaken lightly.

Peers's place was taken by a new manager named Alexander Mackenzie. Mackenzie took the dead man's place at home as well, for in 1855 he married Peers's widow.

Peers was gone, but apparently not forgotten. For years his widow, now Mrs. Mackenzie, brooded over his last wishes. She could not feel easy while her late husband lay in an unwanted grave. Finally, in 1859, a full six years after Peers's death, Mackenzie authorized the transfer of Peers's body to Fort Simpson, where he seemed to have been happiest in life. It was to be a difficult 500-mile journey, much of it over great masses of tumbled ice. But Mackenzie knew the body had to be moved, or he and his wife would have no peace.

Peers's body had been placed in a shallow grave. But the grave had been dug into the permafrost—ground that is always well below the freezing point. When the body was dug up it was found to be in a state of perfect preservation. Those who looked into the coffin said that Augustus Peers looked exactly as he had on the day he died.

The body was placed in a new coffin, and lashed to a sled. It was to be taken first to Fort Norman, and from there to Fort Simpson. A small party of men led by Roderick MacPherson was to accompany the sled bearing the corpse. They set out in 1860.

The first part of the journey was over relatively level ground and it went swiftly and without incident. But at Fort Norman the terrain changed. The sleds now had to make their way carefully through the masses of tumbled ice thrown up by the river they followed. The heavy coffin would have made the sled too unwieldy for this sort of journey. So Peers's body was removed from the coffin, carefully wrapped in canvas, and lashed to the sled.

On March 15, seven years to the day after his death, the party accompanying Peers's body on its journey south had stopped to set up camp for the night by the riverbank. The day had been clear, and exceptionally warm for that time of year. The sun had beat down on the carefully wrapped corpse—and after seven years it began to thaw, and to decompose.

The odor of decomposing flesh soon attracted the attention of the sled dogs. They had not yet been fed and, besides, sled dogs are always hungry. As far as the dogs were concerned, Peers's body was just so much meat. They began barking furiously at the sled. It would have been only a matter of time until the dogs broke loose and devoured the corpse.

The men who were setting up camp heard the dogs barking, and went to investigate. As they neared the sled that held the corpse they heard a loud voice shout, *"Marche!"* Immediately the dogs quieted down. But no one in the party had shouted. And there wasn't another human being for hundreds of miles around.

The voice sounded as if it had come from the sled that held the corpse. Some members of the party, who had known Peers when he was alive, said the voice sounded just like that of the dead man.

"Marche!" is a French word that means "march" or "move." The word was used throughout Canada and Alaska as a command for sled dogs because many of the early settlers of the North were French. *"Marche"* came to mean either "move on" or "go away." When other people, particularly the Indians and Eskimos of the North, used the French word they found it hard to pronounce properly. When the Eskimos said the

word it sounded like "Mush." That pronunciation stuck. Perhaps in movies you have seen or stories you have read about the Arctic the dog sled drivers yell "Mush." Now you know where that funny word came from.

But the word shouted out to drive away the dogs that day in 1860 was the original French pronunciation. It was the command as Peers would have used it.

The other men in the party were puzzled, and more than a bit shaken by what had happened. But they tried to put it out of their minds. That seemed to work. The next three days of the trip were uneventful.

On the fourth day, however, they heard the word *"Marche!"* shouted once again as they were making camp. The temperature had remained below freezing, so the dogs had not caught scent of the body. They were perfectly quiet. The men could see no threat to the body, though it was already dark and there wasn't much they could see. Still, the call had alerted the men that something might be wrong. They moved the sled containing Peers's corpse closer to the camp.

The following morning they examined the place where the sled containing the corpse had originally been placed. All around the spot there were the tracks of a wolverine. Wolverines are exceptionally ferocious and powerful animals. They are also known to have ravenous appetites. The wolverine would almost certainly have torn the body apart if it had not been moved.

The frozen remains of Augustus Richard Peers arrived safely at Fort Simpson on March 21, 1860. Two days later they were buried in the town graveyard.

Those who had accompanied the corpse on its difficult journey were not cowardly or superstitious men. They were not the sort who were prone to hearing things, or making up stories. But they had all heard the mysterious voice coming from the sled where the dead man lay, at a time when no living person was near it.

Several of them had known Peers. They knew of his desire, almost his obsession, not to be buried north of Fort Simpson. They were convinced that somehow the dead man's voice had come back from beyond death, to protect his body until it could be given the burial he had so deeply desired.

The Frenchman's Body

This is one of the strangest stories of the supernatural ever to come out of America. Yet it may be more than a story. A lot of people have taken it very seriously.

The tale began to unfold in 1850, in the woods near Battle Creek, Michigan. Harper Allyn was a rather solitary fellow who worked in the woolen mills in Battle Creek. When he had time off he would go out alone on hunting and fishing trips on the shores of Goguac Lake, near Battle Creek.

Allyn had heard about a man even more solitary than himself. This man was called the "hermit of Goguac Lake." The hermit lived in a small cabin near the lake. He never went into town, and seemed to deliberately shun all human contact. His only companions were an old dog and a spooky black cat.

Allyn's first contact with the hermit was quite accidental. He was hunting when he came upon the black cat that had been cornered by a rattlesnake. Allyn killed the snake, and brought the cat to its owner. The hermit was overjoyed. He urged Allyn to come and visit him anytime.

The hermit, as it turned out, was not at all the sort of person Allyn had expected. He was very pleasant and seemed well educated. The two men became friends, often hunting and fishing together. The hermit said that his name was Stephen Strand. Though he talked about many subjects, he would never speak of his own past.

One night after returning from a day of fishing, a severe thunderstorm struck. Allyn was forced to spend the night in the hermit's cabin.

Allyn was astonished at the way Stephen Strand reacted to the storm. The man had lived alone for years. He was an experienced outdoorsman, yet he seemed terrified by the thunder and lightning. He securely locked all the windows. When the storm raged he paced nervously about the cabin. Allyn got the feeling his friend was waiting for something terrible to happen.

When the storm was over, and he had calmed a bit,

Strand turned to Allyn and made an astonishing announcement.

"I apologize for acting as I have. But I have a good reason to fear the storm. I, the person you hear speaking, am Stephen Strand. But the body you see is someone else's."

It was now Allyn's turn to become nervous. He knew that his companion had the reputation for being peculiar. But that was the statement of a madman.

Strand tried to reassure him. "I am not mad. Please sit down and I'll explain—but the story is hard to believe."

Though he still felt uneasy, Allyn could not resist hearing Stephen Strand's secret.

Strand said that he had been born in the village of Becket Corners, Massachusetts. He had gone to sea at the age of sixteen. By the time he was twenty he had been able to save enough money to return to his home village and marry.

His bride was Molly Lawton, his childhood sweetheart. They were happy enough together and had several children. Strand worked at a store for five years. But at heart he remained a sailor. And so he finally decided to return to his previous life at sea. His wife sadly accepted his decision.

Strand shipped out on a merchantman bound for France. The trip was routine and uneventful. In France there was a delay of several months. Finally the ship embarked on the first leg of its journey back to America. There were several French passengers aboard. The ship was to stop in Ireland to pick up some cargo.

Off the coast of England, however, the ship was caught in a violent storm. The sails were torn away, and it was smashed on the rocks.

"I was below decks when we hit. I was thrown across the cabin and must have struck my head. I remembered nothing until I woke up."

Then Stephen Strand made his most astonishing announcement. "When I woke up I was dead."

Strand described how he felt his spirit floating in the air. All around he saw the bodies of his shipmates. Then he noticed among the bodies that one, a French passenger, was still alive.

Strand said that he was able to force his spirit into the body of the Frenchman—but only after a long struggle with the Frenchman's spirit.

"His spirit fled. But not far. It still . . . lingers. Always has."

Strand was breathing heavily now. Sweat poured from his forehead. "Every time there is a storm, like there was tonight, that man's spirit tries to repossess his body. I am the soul and mind of Stephen Strand. But the body belongs to the Frenchman I conquered on that stormy night so many years ago."

Allyn didn't know what to think. The story sounded utterly unbelievable, completely mad. Yet the man who called himself Stephen Strand obviously believed what he was saying. No one could fake the terror that showed on his face. And to Allyn he did not seem mad.

"Did you know anything about this Frenchman?" asked Allyn.

"Very little. I found some letters and a few personal objects. But they were lost long ago. All I have left of him is this."

Strand reached into his pocket and withdrew a small beautifully made gold matchbox. Engraved on the top of the box was the name Jacques Beaumont. He pressed the box into Allyn's hand.

"I want you to have this. And in return I would like to have a small picture of yourself. You surely must have one."

Allyn protested. The gold box was very valuable. The picture was almost worthless. Strand insisted. "I want to remember you. You're my only friend, and if you listen to the rest of my story, you will know why.

"I, or Beaumont, was the only survivor. I floated to shore on a large piece of wood. Later, when I recovered from my ordeal, I found it was a shock every time I looked in a mirror. I expected to see the face of Stephen Strand. Instead, there was a stranger looking back at me."

Strand told of how he made his way back to America, and to his home in Becket Corners. His reception was worse than he had anticipated.

Naturally his wife, Molly, did not recognize him.

She insisted that her husband, Stephen Strand, had been killed in a shipwreck off the English coast. His body had been found washed ashore. There could be no doubt.

When he told his story, she thought he was a madman, and ran from him in terror. So did his children.

None of his old friends would believe him. Finally he was actually driven out of his hometown by the people he had known all his life. They thought he was an imposter and wanted to have him sent to jail or to the asylum.

The unhappy man wandered around for several years, finally winding up in the lonely cabin on the shores of Goguac Lake.

The story was utterly unbelievable. Yet Allyn felt that it somehow had the ring of truth about it. The man who told it certainly believed it.

Over the next few months Allyn continued to visit with his friend on Goguac Lake, but they never again talked about the past. Allyn, however, did not forget what he had been told. He determined to confirm as much of the story as he could.

He wrote to the newspaper in Becket Corners for information on Stephen Strand. The editor replied that a man of that name had once lived in the village. But he had been lost at sea long ago. His widow and children had moved west to live with a wealthy brother. So at least a part of the story that the man who called himself Stephen Strand had told him had been confirmed.

About a year after the night that the terrible storm had struck Goguac Lake, there was another one. This one was far more severe. The first chance he got, Allyn went to the lake to see how his friend had endured the thunder and lightning. Stephen Strand's cabin was empty. There were signs that a tremendous struggle had taken place inside.

When Strand was reported missing, the area was searched. The lake was dragged. But no trace of the mortal remains of the man who called himself Stephen Strand was ever located.

A curious twist of fate allowed Harper Allyn to write another chapter to this strange story. Allyn unexpectedly came into a considerable inheritance. He quit his job at the woolen mill and decided to spend the rest of his life traveling.

He heard that one of his old friends, Charley Bushnell, was living in Paris. The thought of seeing his old friend, and of visiting the native land of Jacques Beaumont, interested Allyn a great deal. So he made Paris the first stop in his travels.

Bushnell was delighted to see him. He had made a lot of friends in Paris. As a result, he was able to take Allyn to a large number of parties. At one of these gatherings Allyn was introduced to an attractive woman. She stared at him in disbelief.

"I'm sorry to be so rude," she said. "But your face and name are familiar to me."

Allyn said he didn't see how that was possible, since he had never been in France before, indeed had never traveled outside of America before.

"My name is Lily Beaumont," the woman said. "And I just saw your picture last week."

A shiver went up Allyn's spine. He remembered the picture he had given to Stephen Strand, and he remembered the name of the man whose body Strand claimed to inhabit—Jacques Beaumont.

"My name means something to you," the woman said.

"Perhaps," answered Allyn. "I can't be sure."

Lily Beaumont said that about a week ago, a very old man had come to the village where she lived with her mother. The man claimed to be her father, Jacques Beaumont. But everyone knew that Jacques Beaumont had been lost in a shipwreck years ago. True, the man bore a faint resemblance to Jacques Beaumont. But after so many years, memory can fade, and play tricks. When the man told of how his body had been possessed by the spirit of another, that sounded insane. The police came and took him away.

"The only thing the old man carried," said Lily Beaumont, "was a photo of you, with your name, Harper Allyn, written on the back."

Allyn then told her his story of the hermit of Goguac

Lake. Now the story no longer sounded so unbeliev-able. Allyn and Lily Beaumont left immediately for the village where Lily's mother lived, and where the asy-lum in which the old man was being kept was located.

Allyn showed Madame Beaumont, Lily's mother, the gold matchbox that he had been given. The sight of it nearly made her faint. It was the same box she had given to her husband just before he had boarded the ship for his final voyage so many years ago.

Allyn visited the old man in the asylum. He had aged greatly, and was clearly in poor health, yet there was no doubt that this was his old friend, the man who had called himself Stephen Strand.

Strand, or whoever he was, did not recognize Allyn. He did not seem to understand a word of English. Was Jacques Beaumont able to repossess the body stolen from him by Stephen Strand?

As the story circulated around the village, opinions were split. Some people said the old man was an insane impostor. Others who had known Jacques Beaumont claimed they could recognize him—far older, and much changed, but still recognizable.

Allyn did not know what to do. He stayed with the Beaumont family, and kept track of the old man's prog-ress. The old man grew weaker all the time. Finally, word came that he was dying. Allyn came to his bed-side. A priest was there to administer the last rites.

Allyn asked the dying man: "Will you tell me, are

you Stephen Strand or Jacques Beaumont?"

The old man whispered: "In the presence of God, I swear I am . . ." He let out a gasp and fell back on his pillow—dead.

A strange, and unbelievable story. Is it true, or simply made up? The details can no longer be checked. The story first appeared in print just a few years after the events described were supposed to have taken place. It has attracted the attention of psychical researchers, and even of an Indian mystic who wrote it up as "A Case of Reincarnation from America."

12

The Duke Returns

Who is the most famous ghost in America today?

Is it Abraham Lincoln whose spirit is supposed to walk the corridors of the White House?

Perhaps it is Aaron Burr, that controversial character from early American history whose spirit has been reported in a number of different sites associated with him.

Could it be Marie Laveau, the mysterious voodoo queen of New Orleans, who is still seen from time to time, though she has been dead for over a century?

All of these ghosts have their fans. But for my money the best-known celebrity ghost in the United States today is the ghost of the actor John Wayne. Yes, according to some accounts, "The Duke" has returned to walk the decks and prowl the passageways of the yacht that he once owned and loved.

John Wayne, superstar of Western films, died in June, 1979. Wayne had been ill for years. He knew he was going to die. Before he died he spent a lot of time making sure that the things he cared about would be properly treated after his death.

One of the things The Duke cared about was his yacht called *The Wild Goose*. *The Wild Goose* was a World War II minesweeper that had been converted into a luxury yacht. The actor purchased it in 1964, and during the last years of his life he had spent some of his happiest hours on board. Wayne wanted to make absolutely sure that *The Wild Goose* would be bought by someone who would take proper care of it. He wasn't going to sell his beloved boat to just anyone.

The man who eventually purchased *The Wild Goose* was a California lawyer named Lynn Hutchens. It wasn't an ordinary sale, it was more like an adoption. Hutchens had to go through a long series of interviews to make certain that he was "suitable." Finally Wayne decided that the lawyer would take good care of his boat, and the sale was completed.

Hutchens could hardly believe his good fortune. He had always been a great fan of John Wayne's. He never really regarded the yacht as his. It was always "John's

John Wayne

boat." John Wayne's awards and pictures are still on the walls. His books are still in the library. In many ways *The Wild Goose* is a floating monument to John Wayne. That's just the way Lynn Hutchens wants it.

But Hutchens may have gotten more than he bargained for. Just a few months after the actor's death, the lawyer began seeing The Duke's spirit on board.

The first time he saw The Duke's ghost was in August, 1979. Hutchens had been asleep in Wayne's old stateroom. He woke up just as dawn was breaking and became aware that there was a figure standing in the doorway. It was still pretty dark, so he couldn't see the figure clearly. But he knew it was a big man, wearing a broad-brimmed Western hat. He was sure that the figure he saw was that of John Wayne. After a few seconds the apparition was gone.

In October, 1979, Hutchens was sitting in the main salon of the yacht reading. Again he became aware of another presence in the room. He looked into the mirror behind the bar. He saw his own reflection, and the reflection of another figure. It was the same large man wearing a Western hat, which partly obscured his features. But the lawyer was sure that under the hat was the ghost of John Wayne. He turned to try to get a closer look at the figure, perhaps to talk to it. But it was gone.

The footsteps began a few months later. Around 2:00 A.M. mysterious footsteps were heard pacing up and down the deck of *The Wild Goose*. It was not only Hutchens who heard the noises. Others who had been guests on *The Wild Goose* or members of the crew have heard them as well. Later, Hutchens learned that Wayne would often exercise early in the morning by walking twenty laps around the deck of *The Wild Goose*.

The yacht is kept in the harbor at Newport, California. That's where John Wayne also kept it, and it's near The Duke's old house. Once Hutchens was using the yacht for a wedding reception. There were some eighty guests on board. Somehow someone in the crew mistakenly shut off the engine. The boat was allowed to drift. Though the currents and winds should have pushed it out to sea, *The Wild Goose* unaccountably drifted toward shore, and it ran aground right in front of John Wayne's old house.

Hutchens didn't try to keep his celebrity ghost a secret. He told some newspaper reporters, and soon reporters and television crews were swarming all over *The Wild Goose*. He also told some parapsychologists. They came to investigate. They didn't actually see anything that would indicate that The Duke's ghost still walks *The Wild Goose*. On the other hand, they came away convinced that Lynn Hutchens was an honest man. He really believed what he had seen and heard.

Perhaps the lawyer's emotional attachment to *The Wild Goose* and to the memory of John Wayne had such a powerful impact on his imagination that it caused him to think he saw The Duke's ghost. Perhaps others heard different noises at 2:00 A.M. and just thought they were footsteps, because they knew they were supposed to hear footsteps.

And perhaps it's all true.

There's nothing frightening about the ghost of John Wayne. There are no white sheets or rattling chains, no horrible shrieks, or icy touches. If you have to meet a ghost, that's the sort you would like to meet—friendly, well-behaved, and famous.

13

Four Chilling Events

In the 1930s, the local newspaper in Syracuse, New York, ran what appeared to be a funny story. A group of boys went to see a vaudeville show. When they got out it was quite late, and the night was cold and windy.

As they walked past an alleyway a white figure, with wildly waving arms, rushed toward them. The boys were terrified, and too frightened to look closely. They just ran. The white figure chased them for about half a block. It appeared to be aiming at catching one particular boy.

Suddenly the figure fell to the sidewalk. The boys stopped running. After a couple of moments the braver among them decided to go back for a closer look. The "ghost" turned out to be a man's white shirt. It had apparently been starched and hung out on a clothesline. The wind had puffed up the shirt, and it had frozen that way. When it was blown off the clothesline, it held its shape, and looked remarkably like a ghost, particularly to a bunch of frightened teenagers. Everybody had a good laugh from the story.

Three days later the story was given a grim twist. There was a report that the boy the ghostly shirt had been pursuing was killed at a railroad crossing just a short distance from where the incident with the shirt had taken place.

The phantom hitchhiker is the most popular ghostly legend in America. It's the story about the man who picks up a young girl who is hitchhiking. She mysteriously disappears from the car. Later it turns out that the girl who was picked up is really a ghost.

There are lots of different stories about mysterious hitchhikers.

Here's one that comes from the 1950s.

A couple of women were driving toward West Point in New York State. They saw a man standing alongside the road trying to hitch a ride. Though the women would not normally pick up a hitchhiker, this fellow was elderly and he seemed so small and respectable-looking that they stopped. The little old man turned out to be a perfectly safe and inoffensive rider.

He asked to get off just a few miles down the road. As he prepared to leave the car, he said he wanted to thank the women by giving them a little message.

"You see, ladies, I have a psychic gift. I can tell you that within three hours there will be a dead man in your car; also that in January a prominent European politician will be shot—not killed, mind you, just shot."

After that the two women were quite relieved when the hitchhiker left. They were convinced that they had been riding with a crazy man. It wasn't long before they realized that he wasn't crazy.

An hour after the hitchhiker had delivered his prediction, the women were stopped by a state policeman. He told them that there had been a bad accident just up the road. The trooper asked the women to take one of the victims, a man, to the nearest hospital. When they got the badly injured victim to the hospital, the doctors found he was already dead.

What about the second part of the prediction? Well, during the 1950s a lot of European politicians were getting shot.

At the University of Indiana there are some very old buildings on campus. One of them, now a girls' dorm, is supposed to be haunted. There is also a story about how this particular haunting came about.

The building had once been a men's dorm. There

was a medical student who had a room on the third floor. Every so often his girl friend would sneak up to his room, though this was strictly forbidden by the rules.

One night, while she was in his room, the girl and the medical student had a terrible fight. The medical student seemed to completely lose control of himself. He almost went insane. He grabbed for one of the scalpels that he kept for dissection and stabbed the girl in the throat. She died without making a sound.

The medical student then waited until it was very late and the dorm corridors were deserted. He carried the girl's body down into the building's huge basement and hid it in an unused passageway. He hoped that the body would not be found.

However, after the girl was missing for a few days, college authorities got suspicious. They notified the police, and the police began asking questions. They soon discovered that the missing girl had been regularly seeing the medical student. When they questioned the medical student, he broke down almost immediately and confessed his crime. He led the police to where he had hidden the body.

However, the murdered girl's ghost is said to still haunt the old building, which has now been turned into a girls' dorm. At least, that's what a lot of incoming freshmen who have rooms in the dorm are told when they first arrive.

There are lots of tales of people who were mistakenly buried alive. This rather gruesome tale was taken as fact in many towns in southern Illinois.

The event took place about one hundred years ago. There was a young woman who had been ill for several weeks. One day the doctor arrived, and found that she was dead. In those days doctors did not examine patients they took to be dead too carefully. And they didn't take a lot of time before burying people either. The body was put in a pine box, there was a quick service, and swift burial in the local cemetery.

As it happened, grave robbers were at work in the area. They would dig up bodies in search of jewelry or any other valuables that might be buried with the corpse.

On the night of the woman's funeral a team of grave robbers entered the cemetery. It was easy to dig up the fresh grave because the earth was still soft. The robbers quickly uncovered the coffin and pried open the lid.

The robbers were immediately attracted by a large ruby ring on the woman's finger. First they tried to pull the ring off, but without any success. They knew that they didn't have any time to waste, so they decided to cut off the woman's finger to get the ring.

As one of the robbers made the first cut with his knife, the dead woman's arm trembled. Suddenly she sat up in the coffin and opened her eyes wide.

The robbers were absolutely horrified, and ran away so quickly that their feet seemed barely to touch the ground.

The "dead" woman climbed out of her coffin and walked home. She told her astonished family that she had fallen into some sort of paralyzed state. All through the funeral she knew what was going on around her, but she was unable to move or speak. The pain of the knife cutting her finger somehow snapped her out of the state.

Thanks to the robbers, she recovered and went on to live a full life. The gang of grave robbers was never heard from again.

About the Author

DANIEL COHEN is the author of over a hundred books for both young readers and adults, and he is a former managing editor of *Science Digest* magazine. His titles include *Supermonsters*, *The Greatest Monsters in the World*, *Real Ghosts*, *Science Fiction's Greatest Monsters*, *The Restless Dead: Ghostly Tales from Around the World*, and *The Monsters of Star Trek*, all of which are available in Archway Paperback editions. His other Minstrel titles include *Ghostly Terrors*, *The World's Most Famous Ghosts*, and *Zoo Superstars*.

Mr. Cohen was born in Chicago and has a degree in journalism from the University of Illinois. He has lectured at colleges and universities throughout the country. Mr. Cohen lives with his wife in New York.